Sandy Lane Stables

Sandy Lane Stables

Ride by Moonlight

Michelle Bates

Adapted by: Mary Sebag-Montefiore

Reading consultant: Alison Kelly

Series editor: Lesley Sims

Designed by: Brenda Cole

Cover and inside illustrations: Barbara Bongini

Map illustrations: John Woodcock

This edition first published in 2016 by Usborne Publishing Ltd.,
Usborne House, 83-85 Saffron Hill, London EC1N 8RT, England.
www.usborne.com

The name Usborne and the devices ♀ 🎈 are Trade Marks of
Usborne Publishing Ltd. UKE

A CIP catalogue record for this book is available from the British Library.

Contents

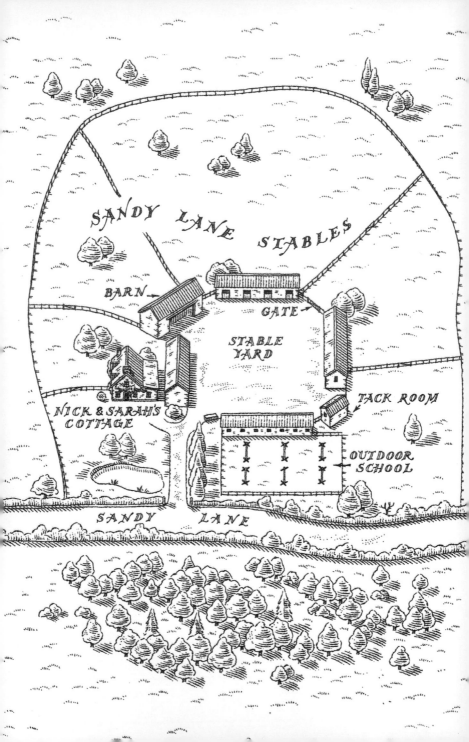

Chapter 1

Heated Words

"I can't, Tom... I'm not riding again!" Charlie Marshall's green eyes flashed angrily as he groomed the piebald pony at Sandy Lane Stables. "Oh, leave me alone, can't you!" he shouted. "I'm not stopping you from riding, and it'll be less competition for you as the star rider here."

"That's totally unfair," began Tom.

Charlie didn't answer, just carried on grooming furiously. Tom shrugged his shoulders and walked away. Charlie felt bad as he leaned over the stable door and watched him. Tom was a good friend, and he hadn't meant to have a blazing row, but right now the subject of riding was very raw.

Charlie thought about calling Tom back to apologize; he almost did, but a nagging voice in his head told him it would make things worse – that Tom would think he'd given in, and the whole business would flare up again. Charlie didn't want that. Nothing anyone could do, nothing anyone could say, would make him change his mind. He wasn't getting back into the saddle, and that was that. It was only the second week of the summer holidays too – whatever was he going to do with his time if he wasn't riding?

Charlie sighed. More than anything, he wanted to blank out the accident he'd had at the Elmwood Racing Stables last week, but he couldn't. He'd never forget it. He looked at his watch. Five past eleven. On any normal Tuesday he'd have been racing on the gallops there. He hadn't missed a slot since May. Even in term time he'd still managed to get there before school. But since the accident, he hadn't been back. He'd been phoning in sick, hiding out at his usual stables – Sandy Lane.

Charlie had been riding at Sandy Lane Stables for over two years now – ever since his parents had divorced – and he'd fitted in almost immediately. He'd got on well with all the regular riders, and the owners of the stables, Nick and Sarah Brooks, had been really friendly. In fact, it was Nick who first suggested Charlie might have a future as a jockey... Nick who convinced him he had talent. He was the right size for it too, for Charlie was small for his age.

Once the idea was in Charlie's head, there'd been no stopping him. He'd won a place at the International Racing School for September on the understanding that he came with four months' race work experience. That had been easy to arrange. Josh Wiley, the racehorse trainer at Elmwood, had been advertising for someone to ride out for him for the summer. Everything had fallen into place – as though it was meant to be.

"Hi Charlie! You OK?" Jess Adams' cheery face peered over the stable door.

"I'm fine," he snapped.

"You're very quiet in there," she laughed, tying her brown curls into a ponytail.

"Just thinking," he grunted. "About the accident and stuff."

"Oh." Jess didn't know what to say. "I'm going to my jumping lesson," she muttered, and quickly slipped off to Skylark's stable.

Charlie shrugged his shoulders. For the last week his friends had been trying to get him back on a horse, and now he'd made it clear he wouldn't respond, they seemed at a loss to know how to handle it. Rosie and Jess pretended nothing had happened; Kate and her brother Alex avoided the subject; and Izzy – well, even Izzy seemed too busy with her horse, Midnight, to talk about it. Charlie guessed he made them uneasy, and that didn't make him feel too good. Maybe he needed a break from horses, or to get away from it all. But how? How was that going to be possible when he was living at Sandy Lane for the summer?

It had seemed such a good idea back in May when he'd arranged to board at the stables for the holidays. His mother was going to Florida with her new boyfriend, Jeff, and had wanted Charlie to go with them. But that would have meant giving up everything – his race training, the Colcott Show, the August Holiday Show. Staying with Nick and Sarah at the cottage had seemed like the perfect solution. And, as Sarah was pregnant, Nick needed extra help. Charlie's mother had readily agreed to it. She had always supported him all the way with his riding.

Charlie led Pepper out of his stable and held his head while the rider mounted. Nick was taking a training session in the outdoor school right now. With all the summer shows coming up, excitement was high. But as Pepper plodded off to join the back of the string of horses, Charlie felt only relief that he wasn't taking part. He looked around him. The yard was almost empty. It was a hot July day, but Charlie felt unnaturally cold. He shivered as images of the accident invaded his thoughts. He closed his eyes... the horse walked through the gate... the grass fell away and they stretched out into a gallop. The trees flashed past in a whirl of green. Pounding hooves rang in Charlie's ears and a lurching, sickening feeling spiralled around his stomach. The horse collapsed into nothing and...

"Charlie, Charlie. Are you listening to me?"

Charlie was brought back to earth with a bump by the sound of Tom's voice as it echoed around the yard.

"What? Yes, I'm listening," he answered.

"OK. Then do it," Tom urged.

"What?" Charlie looked puzzled.

"You didn't hear?" Tom tried again. "Go and tack up Napoleon. Let's go out for a ride. Come on, it'll be fine."

Charlie couldn't help feeling irritated. Tom was the only one who hadn't stopped hassling him. "No thanks," he said, grimly. "Like I said, I'm not riding."

And Charlie walked away. Tom didn't seem to understand anything. But then, how could he expect Tom to get what he was going through? How could any of them, when he hadn't told them the true story of what had happened at the racing stables?

Charlie wandered down the driveway. He stopped by the outdoor school and watched as Kate positioned Feather at the wall and neatly jumped over. The rest of his friends were there – Alex, Izzy, Rosie and Jess. All the regular riders were practising hard. But not Tom. He ought to find his friend and apologize.

Quickly, Charlie strode back up the drive and looked in the stables. Tom was in Chancey's stable, picking out one of his horse's hooves.

"Hi, Tom." Charlie spoke gruffly, digging his hands deep into his pockets.

Tom looked up, startled, causing Chancey to edge away. "What is it now?" he asked crossly.

"I'm sorry about earlier," Charlie started.

"That's OK." Tom shrugged, but Charlie could tell his feelings had been hurt. "Go and get Napoleon and we'll go out. Let's forget what was said."

Charlie felt Tom was pushing him. "I can't," he said, trying to stay calm. "I'm not ready. Look," he tried again, "why don't we take the afternoon off – go down to the swimming pool or something. What do you say?"

"Some other time, Charlie," Tom answered him abruptly. "I've got to train Chancey this afternoon. We need to practise if we're going to be ready for the Colcott Show next week, and you ought to be doing the same."

"I've told you – the last thing I feel like doing right now is riding," Charlie said, the anger rising in his throat in spite of himself. "And if you can't understand that, then..."

"Then what?" Tom challenged him.

"Forget it." Charlie thrust his hands deep into his pockets and stared into the distance.

"Look, Charlie," Tom said, more kindly this time. "You've got to pull yourself together. You've had a whole week to get back on a horse and you still haven't done anything about it. I hate to say this but everyone's losing patience with you."

"Oh yeah?" Charlie shouted. "Like who?"

"Like Nick... like Sarah, like just about all of us at Sandy Lane," Tom said. "I know you had a bad fall, but you weren't even hurt – no broken bones or anything. Get back on a horse and get over it. Stop feeling sorry for yourself."

Charlie looked ready to explode. "Sorry for myself? Who do you think you are?"

Tom shrugged his shoulders. "I'm not trying to wind you up," he said quickly. "But if you're not riding soon, Josh Wiley will find someone else to ride out for him and you won't get into racing school without the experience. I can't let you throw your place away like some loser."

Charlie stared at Tom in disbelief. He'd tried to apologize, and his apology had been thrown back in his face. Without another word, he swung around and strode across the yard to Nick and Sarah's cottage. Marching into the kitchen, Charlie slammed the back door shut behind him. Finding himself alone, inside, he leant against the door and let out a huge sigh. Now his entire brave facade collapsed. He felt so tired... tired of all the lies he was telling. And he had a throbbing headache, a dull ache right behind his eyes.

A bad fall, Tom had called it. If only he knew the truth. Let them all think he was a loser – that was a fitting punishment for what he'd done.

Charlie stumbled into the hallway, knocking the black labrador, Ebony, as he passed. Ebony yelped and looked up at him reproachfully.

"I'm sorry. I'm so sorry." Swiftly Charlie knelt, patting the dog's head. "I didn't mean to take it out on you."

Chapter 2

The Nightmare

Charlie slept restlessly. The rhythmic drumming of horses' hooves pounded in his head as he leaned forward in the saddle. On and on he galloped, the wind biting into his face. The ground dropped away as the other horses rode past. Charlie felt a sense of urgency rising in his throat, almost choking him, as he shielded himself from the mud spray.

One more crack from the whip... one more nudge from his heels. Nearer and nearer they flew, closer to the spot.

"Stop, stop!" he cried now. But every tug on the

reins seemed to send the racehorse faster and faster, until Charlie's head was reeling. Furiously, they raced across the turf to the brow of the hill. Just over the top and down the side. Charlie's heart was in his mouth. He knew what was coming next, and yet he couldn't stop it. Closer and closer, nearly there now.

And then, suddenly, the black thoroughbred was dropping away, falling... falling... falling. The glint of the horses' racing plates ahead of him was all that Charlie saw as he hit the ground, tucking himself into a neat ball as he rolled, over and over...

You idiot... you silly fool... you must have been riding too fast... it was your fault... You made it happen.

Charlie sat up rigid, the words echoing in his ears. His bedclothes were wringing wet; his heart was banging away. It was only a dream, he told himself, the same dream that he'd been having for a week now.

He looked at his watch. No point in trying to get back to sleep – he'd told Nick he'd help him bring in the horses at seven thirty.

Throwing back the duvet, Charlie jumped out of bed and struggled into his clothes. Quickly, he went downstairs to the kitchen. Sarah was already up and, as Charlie appeared in the kitchen, she looked up, surprised.

"Hi, Charlie, you're early," she said.

"I couldn't sleep, I– I–" Charlie didn't know what to say.

"Do you want to talk?" Sarah suggested gently.

"I don't know," he hesitated, then stopped himself. Hadn't Tom already told him that everyone was losing patience with him? Sarah had enough on her plate with a baby on the way, without being burdened with his problems too. Yet Charlie desperately needed to talk to someone.

"Come on," Sarah urged. "I couldn't sleep either. The baby's been kicking all night," she added, patting her huge belly.

"OK, thanks." Charlie sat down at the kitchen table as Sarah filled two mugs with tea.

"Just over a month to go now," she said, laughing

as she handed one to Charlie and eased herself down onto the chair. "I can't wait to be a normal size again." She rubbed her eyes.

"Start at the beginning, Charlie? And don't worry about boring me. I'm happy to listen if it will stop you drifting around the yard as if the world's come to an end."

"If that's another lecture coming, then I don't want to hear it," Charlie said, defensively. "Tom's given me enough grief already."

"No, it's not a lecture," Sarah said. "I'm not going to talk. You are."

"Well." Charlie stared across the room at the morning light streaming in through the windows. "I wish it was as simple as everyone seems to think," he began. "I wish it *was* just a case of getting back on a horse. But I can't seem to get the accident out of my head. It wasn't like all the other times I've fallen; there've been loads of those. This is totally different. It's like nothing I've ever felt before." He was trying to explain, but he knew he was waffling.

Sarah looked at him. "Go on," she encouraged.

"I thought I was all right at first," he started again. "It was only when I got back to the racing stables after the ride that I realized I wasn't, that I'd been scared. It's like the feeling you get on a roller coaster – you go up and down and upside down, and all the time your heart is thumping. You're wondering what's coming next, and yet you know you're safe because it's all programmed. It's not like that when you're riding. When you're riding, you're the one in control."

"You've been thinking about this too much," Sarah said, gently.

"I know." Charlie held his head in his hands.

Sarah looked across at Charlie. His blond hair flopped forward, masking his face, making it hard for her to read anything in his expression.

"I understand what you're going through," she said, soothingly. "And you're right – when you're riding, you are the one in charge, which is why you have to be completely sure about what you're doing.

That shouldn't scare you. Josh Wiley wouldn't have taken you on if he didn't think you were up to it. You know Nick has complete confidence in your riding."

Charlie looked up. His face was pale and drawn, his mouth pinched and thin.

"You'll find a lot of people go through this at some point in their riding careers," Sarah went on. "Lots of riders have falls, falls that scare them, terrify them even. But a true horseman doesn't give in. You *must* ride again."

Sarah sat quietly, waiting for a response. When it didn't come, she leaned forward.

"Charlie," she started. "Is there something you're not telling us?"

Charlie gulped. This was the perfect opportunity to let it all out. Sarah would understand, wouldn't she? Surely she would.

"I know it's been hard for you since the divorce," Sarah started again. "And it must be difficult seeing your mother with someone else, but you have to start rebuilding your life now. She'll be home from

Florida soon and then things will be back to normal. She's not away for long. It'll all be fine."

Charlie didn't know what to think. Sarah had totally misread his discomfort if she thought he was still worried about his parents' divorce – that was the last thing on his mind. He felt like screaming out in frustration. Instead, he spoke in a calm and reasonable manner.

"Nick thinks I'm making a mountain out of a molehill, doesn't he?" he said.

"No," Sarah said, hesitantly. "It's just that he can't understand why you're not riding again. He tried everything to get you on Napoleon last week, and when you wouldn't, he felt baffled and it upset him."

Charlie didn't know what to say.

"Listen, I think that's him moving about upstairs," Sarah said, getting up. "Let's wrap this up while I make some more tea." She opened a tin and got fresh teabags out.

"Hi everyone. What's going on here?"

Before Charlie knew it, Nick was in the kitchen,

sitting down at the table. "You going over to the racing stables this morning then, Charlie?" he asked, a little too casually.

"Nick," Sarah said pleadingly, shooting him a look that clearly asked him to be quiet. Nick held up his hand to silence her, waiting for Charlie's response.

"No," Charlie said, obstinately.

"And why not?" Nick asked.

"You know why not," Sarah said, intervening on Charlie's behalf.

"I told Josh I'd let him know when I'm going back," Charlie said in a defensive voice. He felt incredibly guilty, knowing that he wasn't telling Nick the whole truth.

"You said that last week, Charlie," Nick said, more gently this time.

"Does it matter?" Charlie raised his voice.

"Yes, it does. You should be trying to ride again." Nick's voice was calmly controlled.

Charlie bit his tongue. And then he let go. "I've told you," he snapped. "I'm not up to it yet." He got up and walked out of the kitchen, slamming the door behind him. As he stepped into the hall, he stopped for a second and took a deep breath. He ought to go back and apologize. But now he could hear Sarah and Nick talking again.

"Think, Nick," Sarah was saying. "We have to give him time to come to terms with everything. You of all people should understand."

"And just what do you mean by that?" Nick answered, crossly.

"Do you need it spelt out?" Sarah replied. "You know what I'm referring to."

"And you know I don't like talking about my old racing days. We're not discussing me here." Nick raised his voice. "It's Charlie we have to think about. He has to start pulling himself together."

Charlie stood still in the hall, rooted to the spot. At the sound of the kitchen door beginning to open, he made a quick exit upstairs. He'd heard enough. Nick and Sarah never normally argued and now, because of him, they were angry with each other.

Charlie closed the bedroom door behind him. He couldn't keep disrupting everything. He had to work out a way to get himself riding again, or give up Sandy Lane altogether.

Chapter 3

Another Try

As Sandy Lane was right by the beach, it was the perfect place to ride in summer, and that morning the yard was flooded with extra riders. Charlie found himself running around, grooming, tacking up and taking bookings. It wasn't until eleven o'clock that he found time for a rest, and sat down on the hay bales by the big barn.

"Jess, do you need help with Skylark?" he called, seeing her struggling to pull her pony's head up from the grass.

"No, I'm OK thanks Charlie," she called back,

fumbling with the girth.

"Fine," Charlie answered. He really wanted everyone to be ready so the yard would be quiet again.

Eventually everything seemed to be under control – the ponies were tacked up, the riders mounted, and a string of horses made its way out of the yard. Charlie breathed a sigh of relief as he watched the retreating figures.

As the morning sun bore down on him, Charlie looked across to where Chancey was kept. His stable door stood open. Tom was probably inside, but Tom had ignored him all morning. In fact, they hadn't talked since their argument. Charlie was in a quandary. He'd made up his mind to try to ride, and he wanted to ask Tom for help. But that would mean apologizing for yesterday's argument, and he couldn't make himself do that.

He looked at his watch. Ten past eleven. The ride wouldn't be back for a good hour and a half – just enough time to take a horse out. It was now or never. He just had to say sorry. Slowly, Charlie eased himself off the hay bales.

"Tom," he called.

No answer. Tom clearly wasn't going to make things easy for him. Charlie took a deep breath and crossed the yard.

He called again and peered into the gloom of Chancey's stable to find Tom, frantically brushing away at the chestnut horse's tail.

"What is it?" Tom asked, brushing the hair out of his eyes as he squinted into the brilliant sunshine outside. "I thought you'd said all you wanted to say yesterday."

"I know you're mad at me," Charlie began, "but I've changed my mind. I think I do want to try and ride again."

"So?" Tom looked angrily at Charlie. He seemed more annoyed than pleased by the news. It wasn't the reaction Charlie had been expecting.

"Let's go for that ride you promised me yesterday?" Charlie asked, trying to make light of the situation.

"You've got a nerve, haven't you? Changing your

mind like that," Tom answered him.

"It doesn't sound great, I know," Charlie said, biting his tongue to stop a sharp retort. If he was going to get Tom on his side, he'd have to be as conciliatory as possible. "But you were right. I've got to try and pull myself together."

Tom looked uncertain. "I'm taking Chancey down to the beach for a good hard gallop to muscle him up. I suppose you can come too if you like," he said grudgingly.

Charlie gulped. A good hard gallop was the last thing he felt like.

"Nick's just gone out," Tom went on. "So you'd better ask Sarah if you can take out Napoleon."

"But Tom, I'm not sure if..." Charlie started.

Tom held up his hand. "I'm sure she'll let you."

"OK." Charlie was hesitant. He'd wanted to tell Tom that he was suddenly getting cold feet again, but Tom had interrupted him.

"Go on then," said Tom.

Charlie felt beads of sweat rising on his forehead

as he hurried across to the cottage. He felt embarrassed as he walked into the kitchen. He'd only been saying to Sarah that morning that he wouldn't ride. What would she say?

Sarah was quietly composed as Charlie made his request. "Are you sure about this?" she asked. "Tom hasn't put you up to it, has he?"

"No, it's completely my decision," Charlie answered firmly.

"OK then." She seemed surprised. "If you're sure you're ready for it, then of course it's fine for you to take Napoleon out. You're a competent rider. Nick won't have a problem with that. It's just that after everything you said this morning–"

"I know, I know," Charlie answered, cutting her off mid-sentence.

"That's settled then. See you later."

Charlie nodded and tried to force a smile onto his face.

"All agreed?" Tom asked as he saw Charlie approaching. Charlie nodded.

"Great. I'll get Chancey ready and we'll be off."

Tom disappeared, leaving Charlie to tack up his mount. Charlie made his way to Napoleon's stable.

"You have to help me through this," Charlie said to the big, bay horse. "I'm relying on you to look after me."

Napoleon looked around him and blew through his nostrils as if he was bored.

"It's all right for you," Charlie said, reaching for the saddle and bridle. The stable felt oppressively hot and still, and Charlie had an empty, gnawing feeling in the pit of his stomach.

"There's a boy," he whispered, gently sliding the bridle over Napoleon's head. He reached up to place the saddle on the horse's back and pulled the girth round. As he fastened the buckle, he realized he was shaking. He stood up straight, stopping for a moment to fiddle with Napoleon's forelock – anything to put off the moment when he'd have to go out of the stable and mount.

"It'll be OK. It'll be OK," he told himself and then,

in a daze, he led Napoleon out of the stable. Before he could change his mind, he was following Tom out of the yard, through the gate and into the dusty fields at the back of the yard. He felt giddy as he watched Tom spring neatly into Chancey's saddle.

"Ready? Let's start," said Tom firmly.

"I think I'll just walk Napoleon over to the trees," Charlie said, after a moment, and playing for time. "It'll be easier over there."

"OK." Tom was adjusting his stirrup, and seemed not to notice Charlie's discomfort.

Charlie didn't know why he felt so ill at ease. He'd ridden Napoleon so many times. He didn't even bear any similarity to the racehorse. Big, solid, reliable Napoleon – how could he be scared of riding him? And yet he was.

Napoleon seemed to sense that something was wrong now they had crossed the field. He was getting fidgety, turning on his toes and pirouetting madly, making it difficult for Charlie to get his foot into the stirrup. Every time Charlie went to spring up, Napoleon moved away again. The ground started spinning. Charlie's head was reeling. It was as though he was seeing everything double. He felt dizzy and suddenly very numb. He couldn't think. He couldn't stop thinking. His mind was in a whirl as everything came flooding back – the high-pitched whinny, the thundering hooves, the crashing fall – they all echoed around his head.

Charlie had an overwhelming feeling that he was going to be sick as he leaned against the horse. He felt like he wasn't really there, and yet he could hear Tom calling his name.

"Charlie, are you OK? You've gone very green." Tom's voice snapped him to his senses.

"I don't feel too good. I don't think I can come out with you today after all."

Charlie felt groggy as he reached up to touch his forehead. "I'm just tired. I didn't sleep last night. It must all be beginning to catch up with me."

"Tired! You're more than tired," said Tom. "Let's go and get Sarah."

"No, no, don't do that," Charlie said hurriedly. "I'm starting to feel better already. Only I don't think I should ride Napoleon this morning."

"You're probably right," Tom said, uneasily.

"You won't tell anyone about this, will you?" Charlie pleaded, embarrassed.

"Well..." Tom was hesitant.

"Please," Charlie begged. "I just need more time. I'm not feeling too good at the moment, that's all. I'll be better in a few days – honest I will. You go out for your ride. Chancey's getting impatient. I'll take Napoleon back, and we'll go out another time."

"I think I ought to come with you," Tom said, uncertainly.

"No, Tom," Charlie said, more firmly this time. "No offence, but I'll be fine on my own."

"OK then," Tom said, slowly. "I won't be long, not more than half an hour."

"See you later," Charlie answered, wearily.

And, before Tom could say anything more, Charlie was leading the bay horse off by his reins.

As he walked back to the yard, Charlie felt ashamed of himself. How could he have been such a coward? As he took Napoleon into the stable, he felt relieved to see that the Land Rover had gone – Sarah must have gone shopping. At least she wouldn't have to know about this.

Leaving Napoleon to his haynet, Charlie hurried over to the cottage. Sarah had drawn down all the blinds so that it was cool inside – a dramatic contrast to the burning heat of the yard. And now that he was alone, Charlie pulled out his phone, biting his lip as he tapped the keypad, before collapsing into the soft cushions of an armchair.

"Hi, this is Charlie Marshall speaking... no, no, I don't need Mr. Wiley. Yes, please could you just tell him that I won't be over this week... I'm not feeling well. I think it must be summer 'flu. Yes, a lot of it around. Thanks very much."

Chapter 4

More Lies

Charlie was still slumped in the chair when he heard the Land Rover roll into the yard an hour later. The others had got back from their hack some time ago, but Charlie had stayed hidden... hadn't answered any of their shouts, not even Tom's. He'd just wanted to be left alone. Now that Sarah was back, he'd have to go outside, or at least disappear up to his room, if he was to avoid facing her.

Charlie pushed open the back door and stepped outside. His friends were huddled over in a group by the hay bales, so busy talking that they didn't seem to notice him.

"I don't know what's wrong with Izzy," Rosie was saying.

"She's being really difficult," Jess added. "Yesterday I offered to help her with Midnight, and she snapped at me – told me he was her horse, not mine – as if I didn't know that."

"Something's wrong," Kate joined in, "but I can't work out what it is."

Charlie felt guilty as he listened to what they were saying. He'd been so wrapped up in his own problems that he hadn't noticed the things going on around him.

"Oh, Charlie, there you are," Rosie and Jess called out in unison. "We've been calling and calling you. Where have you been? Didn't you hear us?"

"N-no," Charlie said hesitantly. "What's this about Izzy?" he asked, quickly changing the subject before they could question him more.

"She's been really odd lately. We're sure

something's up, only she won't say. Do you know what's wrong?"

Charlie shook his head. He thought about Izzy. She'd always been headstrong, but she was never moody for long. She'd been strange with him lately too, but Charlie had put it down to embarrassment about his accident.

"Hi you guys." The group turned round to see the very person they were discussing crossing the yard to join them. Quickly, they broke up, feeling embarrassed that they'd actually been caught talking about her behind her back. An unnatural silence developed that was only broken when Tom joined the group. Once again, the focus turned back to Charlie.

"Where were you?" Tom asked, walking over. "I've been searching everywhere for you, Charlie. Didn't you hear me calling?"

"No," Charlie said, avoiding eye contact and turning away.

"Are you lot OK over there?" Nick interrupted

the group. "If any of you are joining the two o'clock hack you'd better shift – it's about to go out."

Uneasily, Charlie shifted his weight from one foot to the other, hoping Nick wouldn't suggest he join the ride. Luckily Nick seemed to have other things on his mind, and then Sarah appeared at the steps to the cottage.

"Can someone help me with the shopping bags?" she called.

"Sure," Charlie answered, quick to jump to help.

"Me too," Tom added.

"Thanks! So how was the ride, you two?" she asked brightly, looking straight at Tom and Charlie.

"What ride?" Nick asked, suspiciously.

"Well–" Sarah began.

And then Charlie stepped in. Before he could stop himself, more lies were spilling out.

"Tom took Chancey out for a training session in the outdoor school and I went and watched," he explained. "You're not going to believe it, but they jumped four foot!" Charlie looked Tom straight in the eye, challenging him to defy him. Tom watched him warily, but didn't say anything.

"Four foot?" Nick looked from Tom to Charlie as if they were mad. "But Chancey easily jumped that last summer. You'll have to do better than that if you're going to impress me," he laughed. "He's a brilliant horse; he should be jumping four footers easily."

"I know," Tom laughed, uneasily. "I did try telling Charlie that, but he wouldn't have it."

Sarah looked bemused, but didn't say anything. "Well, anyway – the shopping," she started, quickly changing the subject. "Tom and Charlie. Can you carry it in?"

"Do you want me to help too?" Nick asked.

"No thanks," Sarah answered. "Two pairs of hands are plenty. Shouldn't you be getting ready for the beach hack?"

"Yes, I guess I should." Nick shrugged his shoulders good-naturedly and turned away. When he was out of earshot, Sarah looked angrily at the two boys in front of her.

"OK you two," she said, pushing her hair behind her ears. "Inside the cottage. You might be able to pull the wool over Nick's eyes – he's got a lot on at the moment, but you won't get past me so easily."

Obediently, Charlie and Tom picked up the bags of shopping and followed Sarah into the cottage.

"What's going on?" she demanded.

Charlie looked at Tom. Tom looked at Charlie, and then Charlie started to speak. When he did, it wasn't the truth he came out with.

"We didn't want Nick to know I'd been riding yet. You see, I didn't do anything much – I took it very easy. Just walking and trotting. And I don't want Nick to get his hopes up if it comes to nothing."

"Still, it's a start, isn't it?" Sarah said, looking relieved. "Didn't I tell you you'd get back on a horse, Charlie?" she beamed.

"Yes," Charlie said, cringing inside at his deceit.

Tom didn't say a word.

"It's brilliant news," she smiled, ignoring Tom's stony face. "You can't expect miracles straight away.

Good on you, Charlie. I'm so pleased. When are you going out again?"

"Not sure," Charlie said, turning away. "Soon."

"Don't leave it too long," Sarah said. "Or you'll have undone all your good work."

"I know," Charlie said, blushing furiously. Quickly he changed the subject. "I'll bring the rest of the shopping in."

"Thanks," Sarah said. "You must tell Nick you're back riding again. He's away on his advanced dressage training course next week, and you shouldn't be riding all that time without him knowing. Anyway, I'll leave you to sort that out."

Charlie nodded and the two boys trooped out of the cottage.

"Why didn't you tell her the truth?" Tom hissed once they were out of earshot. "All that nonsense about walking and trotting. I've had enough. I'm not going to keep covering up for you. You have to tell them you're not riding yet, or they're going to expect more and more from you."

Charlie was silent.

"Look," Tom started again, more kindly this time. "Just tell them what happened. Tell them how bad you felt with Napoleon."

"It won't help. I have to do things in my own time, Tom," Charlie said gruffly. "Surely you of all people can understand that."

Tom looked unconvinced. "I know I took things slowly when I first got Chancey, but that was different. I had bags of time then. Remember, it's the Colcott Show next week. If you haven't sorted yourself by then, you have to let Nick know you're not going to be riding Napoleon."

"I know," Charlie said, impatiently. "I'm sure I'll be back riding in a few days."

Tom shrugged his shoulders and quickly turned away, leaving Charlie alone with his guilt. If only Tom knew the truth. And while it was easy to *sound* confident in front of Tom, Charlie didn't feel it. He didn't feel it at all. In fact, he didn't know if he'd ever be able to put the accident behind him.

Chapter 5

The Pressure Mounts

Excitement about the Colcott Show swept the yard over the next few days. It was always like that before a show – and Colcott was the first major show of the summer. The riders talked about it all the time. In spite of himself, Charlie found himself equally caught up in it. He was starting to feel better.

That morning, Charlie stood watching Jess and Rosie in the fields behind the yard. He couldn't help smiling at them. Both of them were entered for nearly all the gymkhana events and, fiercely competitive, they were taking everything very seriously indeed.

"Skylark knocked that pole down. Come on, Jess, admit it," Rosie squealed.

"Rubbish," Jess laughed. "Skylark's the perfect pony, she wouldn't make a mistake like that," Jess giggled. "Charlie... Charlie, can you come here?"

And before Charlie knew it, he had been summoned over as lines judge for the two girls. Once more they tore up and down the field, swerving in and out of the standing poles, at a lightning pace.

"See? I told you Skylark's the best," Jess shouted as she crossed the line a second before Rosie.

"Look behind you! You've knocked three poles down again," Rosie said smugly.

"Oh, no!" Jess looked puzzled.

"Instant disqualification." A voice came from behind them. Rosie and Jess turned to see Izzy arriving on the back of Midnight. "Only joking," she said. "Can I join you?"

"Of course," Rosie and Jess said in unison, feeling

relieved to see their friend in better spirits.

"Are you going to try this too, Izzy?" Charlie askcd, with a laugh.

"I certainly am," Izzy answered. "We won't stand a chance in the Open Jumping against Tom and, besides, I wouldn't miss a gymkhana for the world."

Charlie smiled. The Colcott Show was renowned for its gymkhana games, and although there was an Open Jumping event there too, it was on the other side of the showground, so you could really only enter one or the other. Most of the Sandy Lane regulars went in for the gymkhana, knowing that there would be other more varied jumping shows later on in the summer.

Charlie guessed Tom was practising right now. Tom took his jumping seriously, understandably, considering that he'd won the Open Jumping at Colcott for the last three years, and was determined to win again.

As Charlie wandered down the drive, he could hear the gentle sound of hooves cantering around the outdoor school. He peered through the fir plantation, and caught a glimpse of Tom's powerful chestnut gelding cantering easily around a figure of eight course.

Springing up onto the railings, he sat quietly watching, waiting for Tom to notice he was there. But Tom was too engrossed in his riding. Once more around the ring he rode, before he saw Charlie and drew to a halt next to him.

"Hi, how's it going?" he asked.

"Not bad," Charlie answered. "I went to watch Jess and Rosie messing around in the fields. They're fighting out the bending race this year."

"I don't know why they don't try the Open Jumping," Tom said. "They're both good."

"The Open Jumping trophy's got your name on it, Tom, and you know it," Charlie grinned. "Anyway, I wanted to talk to you about something else. I've made a decision."

"Oh yes?" Tom sounded interested, but cautious.

"I don't think I'll enter the Colcott Show after all,

but I *will* have another go at riding... perhaps when Nick's not around next week." Charlie's voice craved reassurance.

"Next week? Where's Nick going?" Tom looked puzzled, and then he remembered. "Oh, he's on that dressage course, isn't he? I'd completely forgotten, what with the show and everything." Tom circled Chancey around. "It seems a real waste to cancel your entry for the Open Jumping when no one else is down to ride Napoleon. It's like you're letting Nick and Sarah down. Why don't you tell them how bad you felt when you went to get on Napoleon. At least tell them why you're not riding."

"I don't know," Charlie said, gloomily. "It's just—"

Chancey tossed his head impatiently.

"I'll take him around once more, then we can talk while I'm putting him away," Tom said, trotting Chancey to stop him getting restless.

A gentle breeze flurried through the fir trees, bringing welcome relief from the sweltering heat. Charlie watched as Tom and Chancey glided easily around the course. Tom didn't show a moment's hesitation as he positioned Chancey at the parallel. The chestnut horse responded willingly to the pressure from Tom's heels, and rose confidently for the jumps. Then it was on to the triple – one... two... three... clear. Now there was only the wall... jump and touchdown.

Charlie shivered. If only it could be that easy for him. The rhythmic sound of cantering hooves sounded around the school as he sat, silently watching. Seeing Tom and Chancey jumping so easily made his pain worse. If only he hadn't been so ambitious, if only he hadn't set his heart on a racing career, then he too might still be riding without a care in the world, instead of sitting on the sidelines only watching.

Slowly, Tom drew Chancey to a halt beside the big oak tree and jumped to the ground. "Sure I can't tempt you?" he asked, offering the reins.

As Tom dangled in front of Charlie the one thing he wanted more than anything in the world, the frustration of the last two weeks welled up. Suddenly he couldn't take any more. "I can't. There's more to this than you think, Tom. The accident – I didn't just fall."

Tom looked serious now. "Huh? Tell me exactly what happened."

Charlie hesitated. He hadn't told anyone the full story. He'd blocked it for so long, hoping that if he never put it into words, it would vanish, and time would heal the wound. But it hadn't. Again and again he felt the ghost of the accident returning to haunt him.

"It's a long story," he gulped. "I really don't know if I can..."

"Try," Tom offered.

"OK." Charlie took a deep breath. "Like I told you, I was riding out on the gallops when it happened. I was on a mare called Night Star. We'd gone through the gate and out onto the tracks... everything was fine. I cantered off in the string, and we moved off in a gallop. The other horses started to overtake us... really fast. We were left behind... I can see it all so clearly," he said, speaking fast in his new urgent rush to unload his anxiety.

"...so I gave Night Star a good kick... to wake her up, and then a bit of a tap with the crop, and suddenly we were following along nicely. One more nudge, I thought to myself. We were galloping fast... and getting faster... faster..."

Charlie's eyes glazed over as he felt himself back inside his memory. "And then, we were crashing to the ground. We had fallen... I don't know what happened," he said, vaguely. "It's a blur – all I could see was this horse sprawled on the ground, not moving. I didn't know what to do. No one had seen me fall. When they came back to find out what had happened, I understood. The horse was... was dead... I killed her."

"You mean the horse actually DIED?"

Charlie nodded.

Tom was shocked. "I don't know what to say. Why? How? What on earth did you do to her?" he demanded, the questions tumbling out one after the other in his confusion.

"I didn't do anything, Tom." Charlie was angry. "We weren't going any faster than normal – even if O'Grady said we were."

"O'Grady?" Tom looked even more puzzled. "Who's O'Grady?"

"The head lad at Elmwood Stables," Charlie murmured. "He went berserk... shouted that I was a fool and that I must have been riding too fast. All my fault, he said. Night Star was his favourite horse, you see. He was really upset."

Tom's face creased with concern. "I'm not surprised," he muttered. The words were too much for Charlie, and he exploded.

" *'I'm not surprised.'* Is that all you can say? I should have known you wouldn't understand. Can't you see what I'm going through? I feel so bad."

Tom looked uneasy, as he struggled with his thoughts. "I can't help my reaction. What would you say if I told you Chancey had died when I was riding him? What did Josh Wiley say?"

"I couldn't face him," Charlie said, calmer now. "I don't know if he'd even want me back. I haven't been to the stables since. I couldn't bear to."

"You need to see him," Tom began.

"No." Charlie was adamant.

"Well, at least tell Nick and Sarah about it."

"No way. Not me, not you. NO ONE tells Nick and Sarah."

Tom looked startled at Charlie's vehemence. Equally angry, he answered. "I can't solve this for you, Charlie. If you're not going back to Elmwood, and you're not telling Nick and Sarah, then this will hang over you forever."

Furious, Charlie started to walk away. Then he briefly looked back. "Don't tell anyone," he called. Tom stared silently at him, deeply worried.

Charlie headed off, unsure of his friend's loyalty.

Chapter 6

Unexpected Advice

Charlie stood at the Elmwood Racing Stables gates. Why had he told Tom the truth? It was surely a massive mistake. Now, Nick and Sarah would know... Soon, everyone at the yard would know his guilty secret.

He gazed into the Elmwood yard. He'd come here to talk to Josh Wiley, fighting his total reluctance to go into the stables. Horse after horse was led out from the boxes. The yard looked busy and professional; owners stood around examining their horses. Charlie felt drawn to the glamour of it all, and equally intimidated.

A clock chimed the time. Nine o'clock. The horses would be off to the gallops soon. In spite of himself, Charlie felt a thrill of excitement. The jockeys would mount and lead off.

He watched a boy his own age swing easily into the saddle of a beautiful grey. He felt envious. Once, not long ago, he'd been part of this world.

Then he saw Josh Wiley stride across the yard, calling out instructions to the jockeys. He was obviously busy... too busy to talk. Charlie felt that he shouldn't have come. He sighed, turned away and left the yard.

As he walked up the Sandy Lane drive, he saw Izzy leaning against Midnight's stable. It was late afternoon, and most of the riders were in lessons. Charlie called her name but Izzy didn't reply. He desperately wanted to see a friendly face, but she didn't seem to want to talk to him.

As he got nearer, he realized why. She looked as though she'd been crying. Her face was dirty and smudged and she shot him a look that clearly said she wanted to be alone.

"Are you OK, Izzy?" he asked, ignoring her reproachful look.

"Do I look OK?" she asked through gritted teeth, fiercely wiping a sleeve across her eyes and pushing her hair back from her face. "I'm fine. It's nothing. What's wrong with you anyway?"

"Oh, you know, the usual – the accident and all that." Charlie found his eyes watering.

Something in Izzy seemed to snap. She glared at him. "I can't believe I'm still hearing this," she said angrily. "You think you're the only one who's got problems? Why don't you take a look around?"

"What do you mean?" Charlie said.

"If you stopped wallowing in self pity, and thought about someone else for once, you'd see some of us are miserable too. Don't you realize you're being a complete pain? You fell off a horse. So what?" she cried, the anger rising in her throat. "Do you ever stop to think that something might be wrong with me, for instance?"

"OK, what *is* wrong with you?" asked Charlie, and Izzy let it all spill out.

"Oh, only that I've just got five weeks left with Midnight, that's all, and then I go... yes, I got into boarding school, if any of you had cared to ask. I got my place at Whitecote."

"But you wanted to go to boarding school, Izzy. It was all you talked about last year." So this was why Izzy had been so strange, and he'd thought it was because of him.

"I do want to go," Izzy answered. "It's a fantastic school; it's the best. But it seemed so far off when I sat the entrance exam. I didn't think what I'd feel like leaving Midnight behind," she said, choking with tears. "Anyway, obviously your life is far more important than mine," she added sarcastically. "I can't believe how everyone's pandering to you. It makes me sick. I mean you only fell. It's not as though the horse died or anything, is it?"

Charlie visibly paled. He opened his mouth to say

something, and closed it again.

Izzy frowned. "It didn't, did it? But it can't have done. Why...? How...? Oh Charlie..." she finished, her voice tailing off.

Charlie was silent.

"I'm sorry, Charlie," Izzy went on. "I'm so thoughtless. You must hate me," she said. "I didn't mean any of the things I said. I felt I had my big problem, and you seemed to be going on and on with your little one."

"You're right about the horse," Charlie said. "But it's even worse; it was my fault."

"How can it have been your fault? Tell me exactly what happened."

Charlie sat down on an upturned bucket, cradling his head. "OK, here's the whole story," he went on, his hands shaking. "I was out on the training fields. We were galloping... the horse dropped away beneath me... she just dropped down dead. I was riding too fast..."

"Rubbish," Izzy said straightaway, in a self-assured

voice. "There must be something more to it. You can't kill a horse by riding it. There must have been something wrong with her."

"I don't know." Charlie was unconvinced. "The head lad at Elmwood made me think it was my fault... and Tom."

"Tom knows about this?" Izzy looked surprised.

"I told him two days ago," Charlie said gloomily. "He was really shocked."

"But how can it have been your fault?" Izzy cried in exasperation. "Have you been back to the racing stables to check?"

"No," Charlie answered.

"Then why don't you go and get some answers?"

"I tried that. I couldn't face it." Charlie blurted the words out, his voice tense. "I don't want to, and now I'm worried Tom is going to tell Nick and Sarah, even though I asked him not to."

"Hmm..." Izzy had an idea forming in her head.

"What is it?" Charlie asked, seeing the expression on her face.

"If you're riding again," she started slowly, "Nick and Sarah don't need to know the truth about the accident, do they? That the horse actually died. Come on, Charlie," Izzy cried. "Why not try tomorrow when we're all at the Colcott Show? You could take Napoleon out when there's no one to watch you."

"Hmm." Charlie looked doubtful. "I was going to try when Nick was away on his course, but maybe the sooner I do it the better. And with no one around at all. Maybe that's the answer."

"It certainly is," Izzy said enthusiastically, her own problems apparently forgotten for a moment. "Be determined. We need to talk more about this." And she led him off to the tack room...

Chapter 7

Catastrophe Strikes

The morning of the Colcott Show dawned brilliant with sunshine. Since six o'clock, everyone had been rushing around madly, grooming, plaiting manes and oiling hooves. Charlie and Izzy had concocted a plan yesterday afternoon. Charlie would offer to stay behind and look after the yard for Sarah. That way, she could go to the show, and Charlie would have the chance to take out Napoleon. And it had worked. Nick and Sarah had agreed.

Now it was eight o'clock and the yard was in chaos. Charlie was relieved to see that each of the horses and riders was nearly ready. Not long now.

"Hi Charlie. Have you told Nick and Sarah about the accident yet?" Tom asked as they loaded the last of the horses into the horsebox.

"No," Charlie answered firmly, walking off.

"Hey! You're short on time. Nick's off on his training course tomorrow," Tom called out from the cab of the horsebox. "We'll talk about this later – at the show."

"I'm not coming," Charlie answered.

"What do you mean you're not coming? You don't care enough even to watch?"

Charlie shrugged his shoulders, his jaw jutting defiantly. "I'm looking after the stables."

"Huh! If you won't tell Nick and let him help you ride again, then maybe you should let go of your place at the International Racing School. Give someone else a chance of getting in."

Charlie tried to look nonchalant, but he felt sick at Tom's throwaway lines. Give up his place at the International Racing School? The thought made

Charlie feel terrible. He was glad to see everyone pile into the Land Rover. They'd be gone soon.

"OK, Charlie?" Izzy whispered to him in passing.

"I'll be fine," Charlie said, through gritted teeth.

"Good luck then," she said. "You can do it."

Charlie smiled weakly. "Good luck as well," he answered, as Sarah summoned Izzy into the back of the Land Rover.

"Take down a phone number with any bookings and say we'll confirm when we get back," Sarah called across to Charlie.

"OK," Charlie answered.

"It shouldn't be too busy. I think most people know we're at the show today," Sarah went on.

"Fine," Charlie replied.

At last everyone was ready. Doors were slammed and the horse box drove out of the yard. They were off. The last thing Charlie saw was Izzy's face peering from the window as they drove out of the yard. He thought about what Tom had said. He did want his place at the International Racing School. Charlie hated the way he felt, loathed the sick feeling in his guts. Izzy was right. He had to get riding again.

As he crossed the yard, he stopped for a moment to fill up a haynet. He collected Napoleon's saddle and bridle and dumped them outside the stable, then looked around him. Maybe he should tidy up a little. He knew he was prolonging the agony.

"Pull yourself together," he said to himself. Taking a deep breath, he approached Napoleon's stable.

"OK boy?" he said, looking inside. Napoleon ignored him.

"I'm sorry you're missing the show. It's my fault, but I'm going to take you out for a ride now."

Somehow, saying things aloud helped Charlie and he was starting to feel slightly calmer.

Quickly he groomed Napoleon. Then, just as he was about to pick up the bridle, he heard a car roll into the yard. Sarah was back! She must have forgotten something.

Charlie froze to the spot, not daring to look out over the box. Panic seized hold of him. Then he heard a voice call out, and he breathed a sigh of relief. False alarm. It wasn't Sarah.

"Is anyone around?" A woman's voice echoed around the yard. Charlie, sneaking a look from the box, saw a woman with a small girl by her side, saying "Isn't this a lovely stables, Julia?"

"It looks brilliant," the girl answered.

"There must be someone here we can talk to," murmured the woman anxiously.

Charlie felt really guilty hiding inside the box. He'd heard the enthusiasm in their voices. He couldn't leave them standing there. He took a deep breath, and backed out of the box.

"Can I help?" he asked.

"We wanted to book some lessons for Julia," said the mother, smiling.

"The owners are at the Colcott Show today," Charlie answered, "but I can take a provisional booking and they'll confirm when they get back."

"Sounds fine," the mother answered. "So, tell me, is it as nice here as it looks?" she said brightly.

"It's an amazing stables," Charlie started. "And Nick Brooks, who runs it, is a first class instructor. He used to be a steeplechase jockey before he set up Sandy Lane."

"Really? And the standard of riding's good?" The mother looked interested.

"The best." Charlie felt a total fraud as he spoke. How could he enthuse about it all, when he couldn't even make himself ride? He felt mean, wishing they would go. They were doing a tour of the stables now. Shifting uneasily from one foot to the other, Charlie waited impatiently.

"Bye then. See you next Thursday," he called as they eventually got into their car again.

"Bye," the little girl waved, grinning.

Charlie took a deep breath as they drove out of the yard, and walked across the gravel.

"Now for that ride, Napoleon."

But he sounded more confident than he felt.

"It's OK. It'll be OK," he said to himself through gritted teeth.

The calm that Charlie had felt earlier evaporated. As he reached up to put on the bridle, his fingers trembled. He struggled to do up the throat lash. Now for the saddle.

Napoleon looked disgruntled as Charlie put the saddle on his back, as if he could sense Charlie's unease. Charlie grimaced, fearing his reluctance was obvious. He knew animals could smell fear on humans.

"Come on boy... settle down," he said as Napoleon sidestepped around the stable.

Swiftly, Charlie led Napoleon out of his loose box, through the gate at the back of the yard. He aimed to take Napoleon right away from the stables so there would be little chance of anyone surprising them. But the further Charlie walked, the harder it became to find a suitable place to stop and mount. The trees rustled in the breeze. Charlie fixed his gaze into the distance. Napoleon was jogging by Charlie's side, getting restless, jumping at imaginary creatures in the hedgerow.

"Settle down," Charlie cried as Napoleon started to break into a raking trot, and Charlie found himself being pulled along, before he managed to calm the horse down to a walk. "We'll go on a few more moments, and then I'll get on," he said soothingly.

Charlie's stomach was tying itself in knots. His arms felt as though they were being yanked out of their sockets. Napoleon was sweating up with excitement, his eyes rolling as he jumped skittishly from side to side. Maybe this wasn't a good idea after all. And then a low-flying military jet shot across the sky. Jets were frequent around Colcott, but this one was followed by another and another. Napoleon flung his head high into the air, jerking the reins out of Charlie's hands.

Before Charlie knew it, the horse was off, galloping madly as if his life depended on it.

"Napoleon, Napoleon," Charlie called, desperately chasing after him. Surely he'd slow down in a moment. But Napoleon wasn't stopping for anyone and, as the horse soared over the fence and galloped off in the direction of Larkfield Copse, Charlie realized with a sinking heart that he'd never catch him. Slowly, Charlie drew to a halt, trying to get his breath back. He didn't know what to do. There wasn't anyone at the yard to help him find Napoleon. One thing was certain. He had to find that horse before everyone got back from the show. Nick would never forgive him if Napoleon came to any harm. That would definitely finish his life at Sandy Lane.

Chapter 8

Confessions

It was a long walk back to the yard. Charlie collected his mountain bike, and then spent the next two hours searching. He didn't have a clue where Napoleon had got to.

In the end he went back to the stables. What should he do? He couldn't leave the yard unmanned any longer. He'd have to report Napoleon missing and that meant acknowledging that the horse was well and truly lost.

Dragging his feet, he pulled his mobile out of his pocket and called the police. He gripped it tight as he listened to their advice. It seemed all he could do was sit and wait. So that was what Charlie did. The rest of the afternoon, he sat in the tack room, willing his phone to ring.

And now it was five o'clock. Nick and the others were still at Colcott, oblivious to what he'd done. They'd be back soon. Time was running out.

Charlie sat staring into space. He half wanted them to get back so he had someone to share the burden with, yet the thought of telling Nick filled him with horror.

Charlie looked at his watch. He was feeling desperate now. And then his heart skipped a beat as he heard a familiar engine in the distance. He felt sick as he looked out of the tack room window to see the horsebox return. They were back.

He watched as his friends poured out, laughing and shouting. The yard buzzed with activity. Ramps were lowered, rosette-laden horses were unloaded, and the riders set about their tasks. Slowly, Charlie got down from the stool and left the tack room, colliding with Tom on the way.

"Watch out," Tom said, good-naturedly. "Aren't you going to ask how Chancey and I did?"

But Charlie was already running across the yard, past the horses and riders. Tom's voice faded as Charlie headed into the cottage. He had to find Nick before anyone noticed Napoleon was missing. He poked his head around the kitchen door.

"Nick, Nick," he called, urgently.

"Hi." Nick's voice answered him, and then he appeared. "Everything OK here?" And then he noticed Charlie's red face. "Is there a problem?"

Charlie took a deep breath. "I'm afraid there is. It's Napoleon... he's not in his stable."

"What do you mean – not in his stable?" Nick looked puzzled. "Has someone put him out to graze? I'm sure I saw him earlier."

"No Nick. I'm not explaining properly," Charlie started again. "I-I accidentally let him go."

"You let him go!" Nick looked startled. "How? When? Where?"

"About three hours ago."

"You mean to tell me he's been missing for three hours!" Nick bellowed. "What were you doing?"

"I took him out for a ride, only I didn't get on straight away, and then some jets startled him. He tugged the reins out of my hands and then he just shot off."

"I haven't got time to listen to this," Nick said. "We have to find him. If he gets onto the road there could be a serious accident, anything could happen. How could you have been so STUPID?"

Charlie stood silent, rooted to the spot.

"What's up?" Sarah, hearing the shouting, appeared in the doorway.

"Napoleon's gone," Nick said breathlessly.

"Gone?"

"Yes, gone. Escaped. He bolted with Charlie. We've got to let the police know."

"I've done that," Charlie said, sounding calmer than he felt.

"I'll go out and look for him myself," snapped

Nick. "Where was he heading?"

"Larkfield Copse," Charlie answered.

"I'll take the Land Rover," Nick said quickly.

"Shall I come with you?" Charlie asked.

"Did you give the police Sandy Lane's phone number as well as your mobile? Yes? Then stay here in case anyone phones." Looking furious, he raced out of the back door.

The kitchen door slammed shut before Charlie had a chance to say anything more. He turned around to see Sarah standing behind him.

"I'm sorry," he said.

Sarah looked at him sympathetically. "I know Nick sounds tough, but you have to understand where he's coming from. You should never have taken a horse out on your own – you could have been hurt. We are responsible for you while your mother's away. And what about Napoleon? Until he's back safely, we can't relax."

"I was crazy, I know," Charlie answered. "I thought that... if..."

What could he say? Sarah believed he'd been riding for the last week. How could he tell her he'd lied? Charlie paced the room, restlessly dragging his hands through his hair.

"Please sit down," Sarah begged. "You're making me nervous."

"Sorry. I'll go outside and get some air."

As Charlie stepped out of the door, a sea of faces greeted him. It was the last thing he needed. Question after question bombarded him.

"What's happened?" Rosie asked.

"Nick looked furious," Jess added.

"Are you OK?" Tom looked concerned.

Charlie took a deep breath. "It's Napoleon... he bolted with me," he started. "I took him out for a ride, only I couldn't hold him," he said, embarrassed.

"You took Napoleon out for a ride?" Tom said.

Charlie nodded, lost for words. Izzy stood back from the crowd, the only one who hadn't spoken. Shamefaced, Charlie walked off to the tack room, the unanswered questions echoing in his ears.

Chapter 9

A Surprise Guest

Nick arrived back at the yard several hours later – hours that Charlie spent anxiously waiting in his room. The long summer day was over and his friends had gone home. Tom had won the Open Jumping as expected, and the others had brought back a collection of rosettes from the gymkhana. But no one was really able to enjoy the success. Everyone's anxiety levels were sky high, and Charlie felt as leaden as the eerie light the dusk was casting over the stables.

The moment Nick returned, Charlie rushed

downstairs to the kitchen. He could tell by Nick's expression that Napoleon was still missing. Charlie didn't know what to say.

"Any calls here?" Nick asked.

"Nothing," Sarah said. "I've rung the police every hour, on the hour. They're sick of the sound of me."

Nick sounded exhausted. "I've looked everywhere I can imagine. All we can do now is wait for news. I'll have a shower. I'm sorry I yelled at you," he added, looking back at Charlie's pinched face. "It's because I'm worried."

"I know, and I'm sorry for what I've done," Charlie answered. Nick's kind words made him feel even worse and he felt a lump rising in his throat. "I didn't know what else to do, you see–"

"Not now, Charlie," Nick said, gently. "We'll talk about it later."

Charlie sat down. "Is there anything I can do to help, Sarah?" he offered.

"Lay the table for supper?" Sarah said. "People

still have to eat, even in a calamity, and maybe it'll take our minds off things."

Charlie nodded. In a daze, he counted out the knives and forks against the background hum of the TV. Slowly, he went to the windowsill to get the table mats. It was dark outside now, and he couldn't see anything very clearly in the yard, but something wasn't right out there. Was that a noise? He paused, mats in hand. No, his mind was playing tricks on him. He was jumping at everything.

But there it was again, and louder now. There *was* something outside.

He pressed his face against the window, staring out into the gloom, and had the fright of his life. On the other side of the window, a familiar face peered in at him. Charlie's heart lurched. Napoleon! Napoleon was standing in Nick and Sarah's garden. Charlie gulped. If he was quiet, he might be able to creep around the back and catch him.

"What is it, Charlie?" Sarah said, glancing up from her stir-fry. "You look like you've seen a ghost."

"Sshh." Charlie pointed to the window. "Have you got a carrot?" he whispered.

Sarah nodded at the vegetable rack, and swiftly Charlie grabbed a large carrot and slipped outside.

The bay horse stood perfectly still, munching contentedly at the grass. He had lost his saddle, and his reins trailed, muddy and broken, by his side, but he appeared to be in one piece.

Approaching him slowly and lightly so as not to disturb him, Charlie leaned forward.

"Come on boy," Charlie said softly. "Nice carrot."

Napoleon looked wary but he didn't move. Charlie hardly dared breathe. Then, with a swish of his tail, Napoleon stumbled over and gratefully accepted the offering. Before he had a chance to move away, Charlie had grabbed the reins.

"You bad, bad boy," Charlie said in a gentle voice, relief flooding through him now that the horse was safe. "Where have you been? We've been worried sick. You had me in serious trouble." Charlie turned round to find Sarah standing behind him.

"Thank goodness," she said. "He's back."

There was a sound of feet racing down the stairs and suddenly Nick appeared at Sarah's shoulder, grinning all over his face.

"I don't believe it," he said.

"I don't know what he's been up to, but he's completely caked in mud," Sarah laughed.

Charlie looked properly at the horse now. It was true. His coat was matted in whorls where he must have been rolling, and briars and twigs were twisted in his mane. Still, at least he was back.

"I'll take him back to his stable and groom him," Charlie offered, adding, looking at Nick, "I know I've got a lot of explaining to do."

"We'll talk that through over supper," nodded Nick as Charlie led the horse off.

The thought of telling Nick and Sarah the whole story filled Charlie with dread. But he had to do it. They'd been incredibly patient with him. He owed it to them. It was time to tell them the truth.

Chapter 10

The Truth of the Matter

"That's quite a story, Charlie," Nick said, as Charlie finished. "Now I understand why you wouldn't ride... the way you've been acting."

"I didn't know what you'd say," muttered Charlie. "I thought you'd blame me. I can't believe you're being so good about it."

"If only you'd told us, I wouldn't have put so much pressure on you. Losing a horse is a very traumatic experience, and one I can completely relate to."

Charlie looked puzzled. At that moment Sarah stood up, saying, "I'm exhausted. Really tired. I'll go to bed. I'm glad it's out in the open, Charlie."

As the door closed on Sarah, Nick started again. "Something like this happened to me. A horse of mine, Golden Fleece, died in an accident too, so I know what you're going through."

"Golden Fleece DIED?" Charlie was shocked. He'd heard so much about the amazing racehorse from Nick's steeplechase days, but he didn't realize she'd been killed in an accident.

"Yes, she died," Nick said sadly. "I don't like talking about it. I stopped racing soon after it happened. I remember thinking at the time that I'd never ride again. But I was wrong about that. It just took time."

Charlie opened his mouth to speak, and then closed it again, judging it best to let Nick tell the story in his own way.

"It still upsets me," Nick continued. He took a deep breath. "It happened quite a while ago, but I remember everything. It was a long time before I could truly put it behind me," he sighed. "It's the real reason I gave up racing and set up Sandy Lane. You see, when Golden Fleece fell and broke her leg, I was convinced I was responsible. I couldn't forgive myself. It took me years to realize that it wasn't my fault. Who could have predicted that the leading horse would fall in front of Golden Fleece and bring her down? Who could have predicted she would land so awkwardly? And me? I was hardly hurt."

Charlie saw the pain in Nick's face.

"But accidents do happen, Charlie," Nick went on. "Racing, like any other sport, has its fair share of them, but they're one-offs – chance happenings that we should learn to accept rather than dwell on too deeply."

Nick stared into the distance. "I've made another life for myself now, but you – you've got your whole racing career ahead of you. Don't throw it away."

He stopped abruptly. "I'm sorry. I've got to get on with my reading tonight if I'm going to be ready for this course tomorrow, but when I come back, I'll phone Josh and find out what really happened. Try not to worry. Horses don't just die for no reason. We'll sort out a training programme for you. Try not to think about this O'Grady. He was just upset. I'll get you riding again, you'll see," he said.

"I'm not sure about that," Charlie said, tentatively. "I've tried everything to get riding again, and I don't think I can do it."

"Yes you can," Nick said firmly.

Charlie didn't say anything more as he got to his feet. He felt a whole lot better now that everything was out in the open and he realized how grateful he was to Nick for listening. He got up to clear the plates as Nick went into the adjoining sitting room with his book.

Charlie finished clearing up, wiped the table and glanced through the open door. Nick was looking tired. Charlie felt guilty seeing him trying to keep his eyes open to read.

"I'm off to bed now," Charlie called to Nick.

"OK," he answered. "Hey, Charlie," he called him back. "You'll look after Sarah for me while I'm away, won't you? You know what she's like – she'll start grooming or mucking out before you know it, and with the baby due in three weeks it's important she doesn't take on too much. If only places weren't so hard to come by, I wouldn't be going on this course at all right now."

"Don't worry. I'll do what I can," Charlie answered.

"Phone me any time," Nick went on. "And I'll be phoning Sandy Lane regularly to check on things."

"OK," Charlie answered, vowing silently not to bother him unless there was a real emergency. Nick had been waiting ages to get his place. Charlie didn't want to trouble him with anything that might mess that up.

"Goodnight then," Nick said. "Can you get up early so we can go through rotas and stuff before I leave?"

"Of course," replied Charlie, anxious to help. "Goodnight Nick."

It was a humid night, oppressively hot. Charlie's head felt fuzzy as he went into his bedroom and pulled out a brochure from the bottom of a pile of riding magazines. He lay on his bed, flicking through page after page of glossy pictures.

It was the prospectus for the International Racing School, well-thumbed and worn. But for Charlie, it held a glimpse of what his future might hold. He hadn't looked at it for three weeks now... three whole weeks. Suddenly he had a flashback to Tom's angry words before the Colcott Show.

'If you're not going to ride, you ought to give up your place at racing school... give someone else a chance of getting in.'

Could he believe Nick when he'd said he'd get him riding again? Or should he call the school in the morning and withdraw?

Charlie stared at the phone number on the back of the prospectus.

He wouldn't do it just yet. He'd trust Nick on this one. Quickly he stuffed the prospectus back under the pile of magazines, where it lay hidden.

Chapter 11

Storm Brewing

Charlie woke up the next morning to a very different day from the one before. It was grey... thunderously grey and dark, and the sky had a murky green tinge to it. Charlie was tired after all the emotion of the previous night, and longed to snuggle back to sleep, but knew he had to get up. Nick was off today, and had specifically asked him to be up early to help.

Charlie heaved himself out of bed and crossed the room to open his bedroom windows. A heavy smell of rain hung in the air. He dressed quickly and raced down the stairs to find Nick and Sarah at the kitchen table.

"Hi," Nick said. "Ready to go over everything?"

"Sure."

"I've cancelled all the lessons while I'm away, so it's only hacks going out. Tom's agreed to take care of those. Sarah will be around all the time, but if you could bring the horses in as usual, and give them their morning feeds, that would be great."

"Fine," Charlie said, grateful that Nick was giving him tasks that didn't require riding.

"You'll need to feed the horses at lunchtime too," Nick went on. "But don't let any of them go out for at least an hour afterwards, OK?"

"OK."

"Good," Nick grinned. "I'll be off in about half an hour, so let's get the horses in."

"OK," Charlie answered.

"You've got my mobile number," said Nick, getting up from the table. "And I'll leave the number of where I'm staying on the pin board."

Charlie followed him into the yard, grabbed a bunch of head collars and joined Nick in the paddock at the back.

Quickly, all the horses were caught and put in their stables. As Charlie led Storm Cloud in, he saw Izzy approach. She looked expectantly at Charlie.

"Well?"

"What?" Charlie looked puzzled.

"Is Napoleon back?"

With all that had happened the night before, not to mention all the rushing around that morning, Charlie had completely forgotten about Napoleon's disappearance.

"Yeah, he's back," Charlie grinned.

"Wow." Izzy looked relieved. "I felt so guilty when I heard he'd gone."

"It wasn't your fault," Charlie said. "You couldn't know I'd muck everything up."

"What happened?"

"Tell you later," Charlie said. "I didn't ride, but I will, and Nick's going to sort out a training programme for me. I can't go through the whole story again."

"Oh." Izzy looked a bit put out, but tactfully kept quiet. Then Tom appeared in the yard. Charlie watched as Tom and Nick flicked through the appointments book.

"Charlie," Nick called.

Reluctantly, Charlie ambled over to them. Things hadn't been the same between him and Tom latcly.

Tom stood there, hands deep in pockets. Charlie shuffled as Nick listcd thc rcst of his instructions.

"That's it, then," Nick said finally. "Can you manage it between you?"

"Sure," Tom said confidently.

"Yes, that's fine," Charlie added.

"I'll nip back into the house to say goodbye to Sarah, and then I'll be off."

"OK," they said in unison.

Neither of the boys said anything to the other and Charlie hurried off to Napoleon's stable. Five minutes later, Nick was in the Land Rover, with his backpack stowed on the seat beside him.

"Bye everyone," he called. "See you Wednesday. Remember – call if you need me."

"I'd better get Chancey ready for the nine o'clock hack," Tom said, turning away.

Charlie made his way to Napoleon's stable.

"Hi, Charlie," Rosie called across the yard. "I hear Napoleon's been found."

"Yeah, Nick told us you did well to catch him," Alex added.

For the first time in ages Charlie felt a part of the gang. "He found us really," he said modestly. "I think he knew that the best grass around was outside Nick and Sarah's kitchen window."

"I'm glad he's back safe and sound," Alex said, good-naturedly. "And I don't know about you, but Tom's given me my jobs for the day – four loose boxes to muck out, five haynets to fill, two horses to groom...that should keep me busy," he grinned. "How am I going to get time to ride?"

Charlie laughed at Alex's mock-serious face.

Awkwardly, he turned to Tom. "Where shall we start?" he asked.

Charlie was relieved to find that things ran smoothly in Nick's absence. Sarah popped her head around the tack room door from time to time, but mostly she left them to it. It wasn't until five o'clock that any of the regular riders had time to go out for a hack, and by then it was pouring with rain.

"Typical," Rosie grimaced, looking out of the tack room window.

"Only a summer shower," Charlie said.

"It's OK for you to say," Rosie moaned. "You're not riding in it."

The sentence slipped out so naturally, and Charlie knew Rosie didn't mean it unkindly, but still he couldn't stop himself from visibly wincing.

"I didn't mean it like that, Charlie," Rosie started. "I just–"

"Don't worry," Charlie interrupted her. "I have to tack up Storm Cloud for her rider."

Swiftly he left the tack room.

But as he hurried across the yard, ignoring the rain, he thought about Rosie's words. Soon Nick would be back and then he'd be riding again, wouldn't he?

He tacked up Storm Cloud, his mind straying as he led the fragile Arab mare out of her stable. Patiently, he held her head for the rider to mount, and then he stood and watched as the riders clattered off down the drive.

"Bye," Charlie called, ducking into the tack room and out of the downpour.

The sky looked dark and thundery. Drops of water trickled down his back as he settled down to clean the tack. Not ideal weather to be riding, he thought, trying to convince himself that he wouldn't have wanted to be out on a day like this anyway.

The time passed quicker than Charlie had expected, and before he knew it six riders, soaked through to the skin, arrived back in the yard.

"It was horrendous, Charlie," Rosie called into

the tack room. "We tried to ride to the lighthouse, but it was so windy we had to give up halfway. I'm soaked to my skin. Can you help us with the horses?"

"Sure," Charlie answered, looking at the rain teeming down outside.

Normally he didn't like getting wet, but he was eager to join in and help out and, with a lighter heart, he stepped outside. For the next half hour, he ran around the yard, helping the others get the horses stabled and bedded for the night.

The rain was pelting down, and Charlie was so wet by the end of it that his hair was plastered to his head and dripping.

At last the stable doors were shut and bolted. It had been a long day.

"See you tomorrow," he shouted to his friends across the yard, racing into the cottage and out of the rain.

"Oh Charlie, look what you're doing," Sarah's voice greeted him as he splashed puddles across the kitchen floor.

"Sorry Sarah," Charlie sneezed.

"I think you'd better have a hot shower this minute," she said, seeing how he was shivering.

"Thanks," answered Charlie, gratefully.

He raced up to his bedroom, peeled off his wet clothes, grabbed a towel to wrap around him, and headed for the shower.

He turned the shower dial up full blast. Soon steam was filling the shower cubicle and almost immediately he started to feel better. The hot water nearly scalded his skin. He let the heat seep right into his bones. The bathroom was at the top of the cottage, and he could hear above the gushing shower flow the rain pelting hard on the roof. Charlie felt comforted that he was inside in the warm.

A clap of thunder rang out, and Charlie's face was aglow as lightning streaked across the sky. He closed his eyes and let the water play over his head and wrap round him. Slowly, he let the images of the accident flood his mind. He replayed it... all of it, following it through from start to finish, and this time he didn't allow the panic to take hold of him. The gallops, the horse falling, the aftermath – all the pictures flashed through his mind, and yet he didn't feel that monumental panic.

Taking a deep breath, Charlie stood immersed in the warm water, letting it flood over him and drown out the noise of the gale.

Chapter 12

Stormy Aftermath

Charlie slept well that night... oblivious to the noise of the storm that blew up outside. The rain hit the window panes like tiny hammer blows, but Charlie was lulled into a deeper slumber than he'd had for some time.

When he woke the next day, the storm had blown over, but he was amazed at the devastation it had wreaked. Sticks and branches lay strewn around the yard and, worse still, one of the pine trees lining the paddock had crashed through the end stable. Luckily, the box was empty, so none of the horses had been hurt but, all the same, it was bad news. The sky was clear and a breeze flitted around the stable yard.

"OK, now I don't mean to be bossy, but we've got a lot of work to do in the yard this morning." Sarah looked worried as the regulars gathered around to hear what she had to say. Charlie looked at the equally anxious faces of his friends as they stood waiting for instructions.

"I'll do as much as I can to clear things up," she went on. "But if you could collect up all the debris, that would be a great help."

"Have you told Nick about this?" Tom asked.

"No. He'd only worry, and he needs to be concentrating on the course. If you could all make a start...?" She suddenly sounded weary as she went back to the cottage.

"Are you OK, Sarah?" Charlie said, following her into the kitchen. "You look anxious."

"I'm fine," Sarah breathed softly. "It's just that, well, I wish this hadn't happened while Nick's away.

I can't find the insurance papers for the yard. I remember Nick saying ages ago that he was going to look out a cheaper policy. I don't know if he ever renewed the old one... Argh, I'll kill him if he hasn't got it sorted. I can't find my mobile anywhere, and the landline's down, and the internet's not working, so I can't even email the insurance company. I'm completely stuck," she said in despair.

"It'll be fine," said Charlie, trying to reassure her. "Look, here's my mobile. Call the insurance company and try and call Nick too. If you know about the insurance you'll feel better. I'll go and take charge of things in the yard."

"Thank you," Sarah said appreciatively, taking his phone. "That would be great."

Back in the yard, Charlie was pleased to see everyone going about their tasks with gusto. The debris of the storm was stacked in a pile over by the barn quicker than he'd imagined possible. As Charlie bent down to pick up a couple of branches, he smiled to himself. It was so like everyone at Sandy Lane to pitch in and help out. And then Tom passed by. Charlie turned away.

"How about you come over to my house for supper tonight, Charlie?" Tom offered. "We could go out to the cinema."

"Good idea," Charlie smiled, wishing he'd thought of it first. "Let's get the horses ready for the ten o'clock," he went on.

"OK," Tom answered.

Ten minutes later, the horses were tacked up and Tom was leading the ride out of the yard.

"See you later, Charlie," he said, twisting around in the saddle from Chancey's back.

The horses settled into their easy strides and walked down the drive just as Sarah came out of the cottage.

"At least that's sorted," she called, looking a lot happier than earlier. "The insurance is in place," she went on. "And I spoke to someone about the landline. The phone will be mended as soon as possible. A fallen tree brought the line down."

"Did you get through to Nick?" Charlie asked.

"Yes, he knows about the phone, and he's a bit upset I've lost my mobile – he saw I was calling from yours – so I haven't added this extra little catastrophe to his worry list," she said, pointing at the end stable. "The insurance people are sending a claim form."

Sarah gave a sigh. "I'm worn out after all that. I'll go and put my feet up."

"Is there anything I can do to help?"

"If you could carry on running the yard, I'd be grateful." Sarah smiled at him.

"Sure," Charlie answered, as she disappeared into the cottage. And then she poked her head out of the door again.

"Charlie?"

"Yes?" he looked up.

"Here. I forgot to give you your mobile. And, well, thanks."

"No worries." Charlie felt a warm glow flood through him, pleased that for once he was doing something right.

Chapter 13

Sarah Panics

"I can't believe the landline's still not working, and you don't even have a signal." It was six o'clock that evening, and Sarah was pacing up and down the kitchen, anxiously looking at Charlie's mobile, as if by so doing she might miraculously get a signal. Charlie even took it outside. Nothing. He didn't know what he could say to calm her.

The grey sky shrouded the cottage in a dull, empty light, adding a sense of gloom to the evening. Sarah was looking upset, as gloomy as the sky; Charlie knew she wanted to talk to Nick, but there was nothing he could do about it. He judged it might be best to keep out of Sarah's way. He turned for the stairs and paused.

"I'm going out soon, Sarah," he called. "Tom's invited me to his house for supper, and then we're going to the cinema. But I can leave my phone with you if you like."

"No point," Sarah snapped. "I'm sorry, Charlie," she added. "I don't know quite what's come over me. I wish I could find my own phone. I'm feeling – restless – I suppose, because of the storm."

"That's all right," Charlie answered, hanging around in the doorway. "Look, if you'd rather I didn't go out then–"

"No, you must go, Charlie," Sarah said, firmly. "Will you be all right getting to Tom's house, or do you want a lift?"

"No, I'll be fine. I'm going there on my bike, but thanks all the same. Tom's mum said she'll drive us to the cinema, and drop me back here afterwards."

"OK," said Sarah. "So what time do you think

you'll be home?"

"About eleven?"

"Fine," Sarah said. "But no later, OK? I don't want to sound like an old battle-axe, but while your mother's away, I'm responsible for you." She smiled.

"OK," Charlie answered. Hopefully she'd be in bed when he got back, and no doubt she'd be back to her usual self by tomorrow. Hurrying into the hall, Charlie grabbed his jacket from the coat rack.

"Good night," he called out.

"Good night," Sarah answered.

Charlie headed for the door. Sprinting across the yard, he grabbed his bike and set off for Tom's house.

Sarah didn't know what to do with herself now Charlie had gone. The house was very quiet. Slowly, she walked over to the window and drew down the blinds. Then she switched on her computer to see if the internet was working. She waited. No, it was still down. Then to her horror, a freak gust of wind whistled wildly round the house, and the lights went out. The room was completely dark. She went through the house, trying switches, but it was no good. The power was dead. There was no way of knowing how long she'd have to wait for it to come on again. She was alone, with no light and no means of communication.

She was completely unprepared for the severe pain that gripped her. She tried to ignore it, but the pain grew stronger. Sarah clutched at her stomach. It was like nothing she'd ever felt before. She'd had an ache in her back that morning, but the baby wasn't due for another two and a half weeks – surely it hadn't started already. She groaned and stumbled to the back door, bending slightly to relieve the pain. Tugging the handle, she pulled it wide.

"Charlie?" she called. "Are you still there?"

There was no reply from the yard. Charlie had disappeared, and Sarah's heart sank. What should she do? She certainly couldn't drive with this pain. She tried to think. And then the pain came again, much fiercer this time. She tried to breathe deeply as she gripped the kitchen table, unable to move.

Chapter 14

Ride by Moonlight

Charlie strolled up the drive to the stables, whistling happily to himself. He'd had a good evening with Tom. It had been awkward at first, with neither of them knowing what to say, and the silences over supper had been uncomfortable, but after the film they'd had an ice cream, and by then they'd relaxed.

They found themselves laughing and joking, even laying bets on whether Sarah's baby would be a boy or a girl. The evening had zipped past, so that when Tom's mum dropped Charlie at the bottom of Sandy

Lane, the two boys decided to meet up at nine the next morning. Charlie had been laughing so much that he hadn't realized until now that he'd left his jacket in Tom's mum's car. It didn't matter. He'd have it tomorrow.

Charlie looked at his watch. Half past eleven, and he'd told Sarah he'd be back by eleven. He'd better creep in so as not to disturb her.

Charlie could just make out the shape of the cottage as he walked on up the drive, but all was dark and silent. Stumbling over the doorstep, he pushed open the back door. Silently, he tiptoed through the kitchen and into the hallway.

"Charlie, Charlie?" a weak voice called out.

Charlie's heart skipped a beat. Something was wrong. Immediately he tried the light, but it didn't work. Cautiously he groped his way into the sitting room. He pulled back the curtains to let in the moonlight. Now he could just see Sarah, crouched over the sofa, her forehead bathed in sweat. Charlie stood rooted to the spot in fear.

"What's happened?" he cried, pulling himself together as he rushed to her side.

"The baby's coming," she grimaced. "It's too soon. I'm scared, Charlie. What if something's terribly wrong? I need help. Can you call an ambulance?"

"I'll do it right now!" Charlie grabbed the phone, frantically pressing the button to get a dialling tone.

"It's still not working," Sarah gasped. "Use yours."

The terrible realisation dawned on Charlie. "I can't," he groaned. "I left it in my jacket in Tom's mum's car."

"Then you'll have to go and get help."

"Don't panic," Charlie reassured her. "Stay where you are."

"Does it look like I'm going anywhere?" Sarah gasped, managing a joke through the pain.

"OK... I'm off," Charlie grinned, and darted out of the back door.

The moon was high in the sky, and an eerie white light filtered across the yard, giving a sort of electric feel to the air. Charlie raced over to the barn to collect his bike, and then he remembered. No bike – it was at Tom's. What could he do? He swept a swift glance around the yard. The Land Rover was there, but he didn't know how to drive, and he was too young anyway. He'd have to run for help. He'd have to sprint like mad – the nearest people lived by Bucknell Woods, a good two miles away.

Charlie didn't hesitate. He didn't even stop to think. Madly, he tore down the driveway, his arms flailing out in the still night air. He plunged around the corner of the drive, and sprinted into Sandy Lane. A yellow glow from the cottages in the distance lighted his way and Charlie pushed himself faster and faster until he thought his lungs might burst.

On he raced, until his legs felt like jelly. He knew he was going to have to stop. Unwittingly, he found his pace slackening off until he was going no faster than a crawl. And still the comforting cottage lights were a long way off. He'd never reach them in time. Charlie strained his eyes to stare into the distance, and felt panic seizing hold of him.

He thought hard. What should he do? Maybe he should turn back to the yard and get help some other way, some quicker way. Yes, that was it. And so Charlie double-backed on himself, willing his legs to start all over again.

"Not far now," he muttered as he jogged back to the yard. "Soon be there."

Charlie turned back up the drive, not really having a fixed plan of action in his mind. He took a deep breath and looked over to Napoleon's stable, gnawing at his bottom lip. Cross-country was by far the quickest way to the nearest cottage. He trembled as Napoleon lifted his head over the stable door and whinnied loudly.

And then Charlie knew he couldn't stand there deliberating any longer. Sarah could be in danger... Sarah's baby could be in danger. He'd have to do it.

No time to think any more. Charlie sped into the tack room and grabbed Napoleon's bridle. No time for a saddle. He raced across the yard and fumbled his way into the dark of the stable.

"Easy does it, Napoleon," he crooned.

Putting the bit in the horse's mouth and throwing the bridle on over his head, Charlie fastened the throat lash and led the horse out into the yard.

He gulped hard and clenched the muscles in his cheeks. Then he threw himself onto Napoleon and rode bareback into the silvery night.

"Go!" he cried, urging his horse on. Effortlessly, they galloped across grass, heading for the scrubland. Charlie bent his head low to shield himself from the coastal wind as they crossed the fields.

It wasn't until they approached the overhang of Bucknell Woods that Charlie slowed Napoleon down to a trot. It was dark ahead of them, and Charlie realized it was going to be tough to navigate the thicket. Where the tops of the trees masked the moonlit sky, he couldn't see a thing.

He squinted, tentatively nudging Napoleon on. Which way should they take to get to the road? All of the paths looked identical.

Charlie took a deep breath. The smell of pine

clung in the air as he rode through the trees, this way and that. Napoleon was sweating, excited by the adventure, and he pulled at the reins. Surely they'd come this way only a minute ago. Charlie wasn't sure. His heart hammered in his chest. They were lost in the deepest depths of a wood, and Charlie didn't know which way to turn.

The night was very still. Charlie felt really scared as he listened for a sound in the distance... anything. And then his spirits soared as moonlight streamed through the trees. He could hear a car in the distance. They must be nearing the road.

Charlie nudged Napoleon on, almost sliding off his back as they broke into a trot. The beam from a car's headlights flashed past. Charlie shielded his eyes from the glow. They were at the road. Urging Napoleon on, they crossed it, the horse's hooves echoing on the tarmac. Charlie's eyes streamed with water as the wind bit into his face and they rode faster and faster along the grass verge.

Slowly, surely, the cottages came into view. They

were shrouded in darkness. Whoever lived in them had obviously already gone to bed. Charlie stopped at the first one. He'd have to wake someone up.

Charlie turned to the gate and jumped to the ground. Taking care to tie Napoleon to the fence, he knocked loudly on the door. No answer. Charlie started to panic. He ran around the side and pressed his nose to the window, but he couldn't see a thing. He ran back to the door and hammered his fists against it. For a moment, Charlie thought that no one was going to answer him. Then a dog started barking. That would wake someone up, surely?

"Please answer," Charlie shouted, banging on the door. And then the lights came on. He heard the rattle of a chain and a bolt was drawn back. The door opened a fraction and an old lady peered through the crack.

"I'm not here to hurt you," Charlie said quickly. "But could you phone for an ambulance for me? Please. It's an emergency. I've come from Sandy Lane. The owner's having a baby."

The old lady didn't do anything, seeming not to understand Charlie's words. "Please," he begged.

For a grim moment, Charlie thought that the woman was going to close the door on him... that his words were going to have no effect, but then something in his voice must have stirred her because the next thing he knew, the chain was sliding back from the door and she let him in.

"You can use the phone," she said, pointing to where it sat in the hallway.

"Thank you, oh thank you," Charlie breathed as he grabbed it and called the emergency service.

"I need an ambulance at Sandy Lane Stables... Mrs. Brooks, the owner, is in labour. Sandy Lane, off the Bucknell Road, yes. And the power's down. Please hurry."

Charlie felt relief surge over him. They were on their way.

"I'm so sorry to have woken you," he said to the old lady. "The phones at the stables haven't been working all day and our mobiles are out of action.

I had to ride here." He gabbled the words out.

"That's fine." She had regained her composure. "Would you like to sit down for a moment?"

"No, no, thank you," Charlie was already halfway down the path. "I have to get back." He stumbled over to Napoleon and gathered up the reins.

He led the horse to a clear spot to mount. "I don't believe it... I rode here." Charlie rubbed his forehead with his hands in disbelief, and suddenly the enormity of the whole situation dawned on him. He had managed to ride... actually ride.

Quickly he sprang up onto Napoleon's back.

He didn't want to go through those dark woods again, so he rode Napoleon down the quiet, moonlit road. It was a longer route, but help was on its way. Charlie eased Napoleon into a trot. If it weren't for the image of Sarah's panic-stricken face in his mind, he might even have felt a little thrill of exhilaration. He was riding again!

Chapter 15

A Long Wait

Charlie pushed Napoleon on more quickly and they headed for the stables. The sound of the horse's hooves on the road rang out clearly in the still of the night.

Charlie felt numb as he adjusted his seat to the easy rise and fall of Napoleon's trot. Riding was the easy part now. Not knowing what would be waiting for him when he got back was beginning to prey on his mind. He hoped that Sarah would be all right. As he made the last turn down the lane, he could see a blue light flashing over the yard. He took a deep breath. The ambulance was there – Sarah would be in safe hands. Relieved, Charlie rode into the drive.

He was greeted by a flurry of activity. For the first few moments no one seemed to notice him, but as he jumped down from Napoleon and led him into his box, one of the ambulance men called over.

"Are you the boy who phoned?"

"Yeah," Charlie said, breathlessly. "I live here, I mean, I'm staying with the Brooks' at the moment. Is Sarah going to be OK?"

"She'll be fine, but the baby's on its way," the man answered. "We have to get her to hospital fast. She's been asking for her husband."

"He's away on a training course at the moment," Charlie said. "I'll call him. But we've no way of communicating here; no phones working. Can I come with you?"

"OK, but hurry," the ambulance man said. "We're off now."

"I'll just get the number for his hotel."

Charlie dashed into the tack room, grabbed it,

and locked up the cottage. The instant he was in the ambulance, it sped out of the yard.

Charlie looked at Sarah's exhausted face as he sat down, and she smiled.

The ambulance drove rapidly, blue light flashing, until they reached the hospital. Charlie stood to one side as Sarah was lowered to the ground on her stretcher.

"You'll be fine," he whispered.

"Thanks, Charlie," Sarah whispered as they wheeled her away. "You'll call Nick?"

"I promise," Charlie said.

"Are you OK?" One of the nurses was walking over to him now. "You came in the ambulance, didn't you?"

"Yes," Charlie answered. "Yes I did."

"Mrs. Brooks is going to the delivery room now. You can sit in the waiting room over there."

"OK," Charlie started. "But first I need a phone."

But the nurse had hurried off before he had a chance to ask where it was. Wearily, he went off in search. Heading down the nearest corridor, he came to a refreshments area with a public phone in the corner. He got out the piece of paper with Nick's hotel number on it and dialled.

The phone rang and rang. At last, someone answered and put him through to Nick's room.

"Hello? Who is this? What's going on?"

"It's Charlie... Sarah's gone into labour. We're at the hospital, but she wants you."

There was silence from the other end, and Charlie began again. "I didn't know what to do," he babbled. "I didn't know where to go – you see the phones are still down at Sandy Lane, and I couldn't get help any other way. I'd left my bike at Tom's, and my mobile's in his mum's car, so I had to ride... I had to ride–"

"You're at Colcott Hospital?" Nick said, not seeming to hear anything else. "It's going to take me a few hours to get there. I'll leave now."

That finished the conversation, and Charlie went back to the waiting room. He sank into a chair to wait for news, realizing suddenly how tired he was.

He was exhausted, both mentally and physically.

His eyelids drooped, heavy with sleep. Try as he might, he couldn't stay awake, and finally allowed himself to succumb to tiredness. In no time at all, he had drifted into sleep. In his dreams though, he was cantering through the fields on Napoleon's back... this time not as if Sarah's life depended on it, but for enjoyment – for pure pleasure. And, as Charlie rode on, the ground slipped away beneath him, and it was as though he and the horse had melted into one.

Chapter 16

A New Addition

"Wake up, Charlie…"

Charlie woke instantly and looked up to see Nick standing there. "How did you get here so fast?"

Nick laughed. "It took me three hours. You've been asleep."

"I couldn't help it. I phoned you, then I went and sat down, and then…"

Nick squeezed his shoulder. "It's been a long and exhausting night for you – especially as you rode again. I want to thank you… if you hadn't acted so quickly, I don't like to think what would have happened. I might not be a proud father!"

"What?" Charlie sat up. "The baby's born?"

"We have a girl," Nick grinned. "A healthy, beautiful little girl."

"Wow!" Charlie cried. "That's amazing. Double amazing – I've won the bet."

"What bet?" Nick looked puzzled.

"I bet Tom she'd be a girl."

Nick patted him on the back and laughed. "Let's go and see them."

Charlie had never seen him look so happy.

They hurried down the corridor to Sarah's ward. Just before they entered, Nick turned to Charlie.

"There's something I must tell you," he said, seriously. "About that racehorse, Night Star."

Charlie stood very still.

"I rang the Elmwood Stables..." Nick began.

"...And?" Charlie's eyes widened with fear.

"And it's OK. If you can ever call the death of a horse OK. Night Star died of a heart attack. I hope you don't mind, but I told Josh Wiley what you'd been going through. He was annoyed you hadn't been turning up. It didn't occur to him you might blame yourself. Anyway, it's all sorted now. Josh is as anxious as I am to work out a training programme for you, although that's not strictly necessary now you're riding again."

"Nick, I–" Charlie didn't know what to say.

"The vet's report came through last week," Nick continued. "The horse had a very weak heart – it could have happened at any time. It's very sad, but it wasn't because of you. In the nicest way possible, it was the best place for a horse to die – out on the gallops. Now," Nick said, "I think I can hear a baby crying. And you need to put this behind you."

Charlie looked uncertain at first, and then he found his voice. "You're right Nick," he said. "And… well, thanks."

The two of them pushed open the door to find Sarah sitting up in bed holding the latest addition to Sandy Lane.

Chapter 17

Back at the Yard

Charlie sat tight to the saddle and cantered neatly around the outdoor school.

"Very good," Nick called. "I'm glad those few weeks off haven't made you forget how to ride."

"How could I ever forget that?" Charlie shouted back across the school. He and Nick had returned to the stables that morning to feed the horses, and Charlie hadn't been able to resist getting back in the saddle. Once he was on a horse, he couldn't imagine how he'd ever thought he might not ride again.

"Once more around the school and then I'll be

really ready for my race training," Charlie shouted.

As soon as he could, after he'd got back from the hospital, he'd rung Josh. And Josh had arranged for him to start riding again the next day. Charlie couldn't believe it had all been so easy. He was almost brimming over with excitement about it.

"Now we've fed the horses, I'll go back to see Sarah and the baby." Nick's voice disturbed Charlie's thoughts. "I'll be back by lunchtime."

"OK," Charlie answered. "What are you going to do about your dressage course though?" he asked.

"That can wait another year. There are more important things to think about. I'll be busy, with the baby coming early, and rebuilding the stable. And we have to get you ready for the August Holiday Show, too. It's only two weekends away. You've got a lot of work to catch up on." Nick chuckled.

"Sure, Nick." Charlie grinned.

Calmly, Charlie circled Napoleon around the school and breezily turned him to the course one more time. Soaring through the air, they cleared jump after jump with ease. Charlie was so engrossed in his riding that he didn't notice Tom pull up on his bicycle and stand goggling behind the railings. And then Izzy arrived and drew up alongside him.

"I can't believe it." Izzy's mouth dropped open. "Whatever got him riding again?" The two friends stood mesmerised at the sidelines. It wasn't until Charlie cleared the last jump and drew to a halt that he noticed his two spectators.

"Charlie... what's happened? When did you... how did you..." Tom was flabbergasted and the questions rolled off his tongue one after the other.

"How did I get riding again? Well," Charlie grinned, "it's a bit of a long story."

"Do Nick and Sarah know about this?" Izzy asked. She didn't know what else to say.

"You could say that – Nick was standing where you both are just a minute ago," Charlie laughed.

"Why is Nick back?" Tom demanded. "This is getting mad. What's going on?"

"Give me a chance and I'll tell you," Charlie

laughed. "Go and get Chancey and Midnight tacked up so we can go out for a hack, then I'll explain. You look happier, Izzy," he said to his friend.

"Well, it's good to see you riding again," she grinned. "And I feel better about boarding school now. I'll come home for loads of weekends, and there's weeks and weeks of holidays too."

"Good on you," Charlie called back.

"But there's one thing you've got to promise me," she went on.

Charlie looked worried at first, and then he relaxed as Izzy smiled.

"You've got to promise to text me every day and tell me how Midnight is," she grinned.

"OK! Come on, let's go. Right now I feel I need a good gallop... Hey, Tom!" He called back to where Tom was still standing by the railings. "You're on mucking out duties next week."

"Mucking out duties?" Tom looked puzzled.

"Yes," Charlie grinned. "I won our bet. Sarah's had a baby girl!"

Sandy Lane Stables

A Horse for the Summer

Michelle Bates

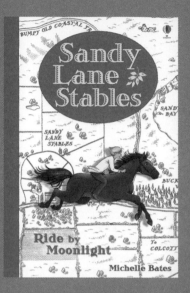

Sandy Lane Stables

Ride by Moonlight

Michelle Bates

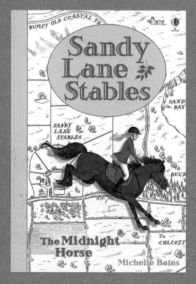

Sandy Lane Stables

The Midnight Horse

Michelle Bates